THE MAN WHO LEARNED TO GIVE

Luke 5:27-32 FOR CHILDREN

Written by Louise Ulmer
Illustrated by John D. Firestone & Associates

ARCH Books

Copyright © 1976 CONCORDIA PUBLISHING HOUSE, ST. LOUIS, MISSOURI

MANUFACTURED IN THE UNITED STATES OF AMERICA

ALL RIGHTS RESERVED

ISBN 0-570-06109-1

In a Galilee town by the city gate
Sat a man named Matthew each day.

He worked there on business for the king.
People brought him their hard-earned pay.

3

The king needed money for new roads and streets,
For armies, and parks, and such;
But sometimes the king's men got greedy
And collected far too much.

"Ten pennies, please," said Matthew
To an old man in shabby shoes.
"You must bring it in by tomorrow
To pay the king his dues."

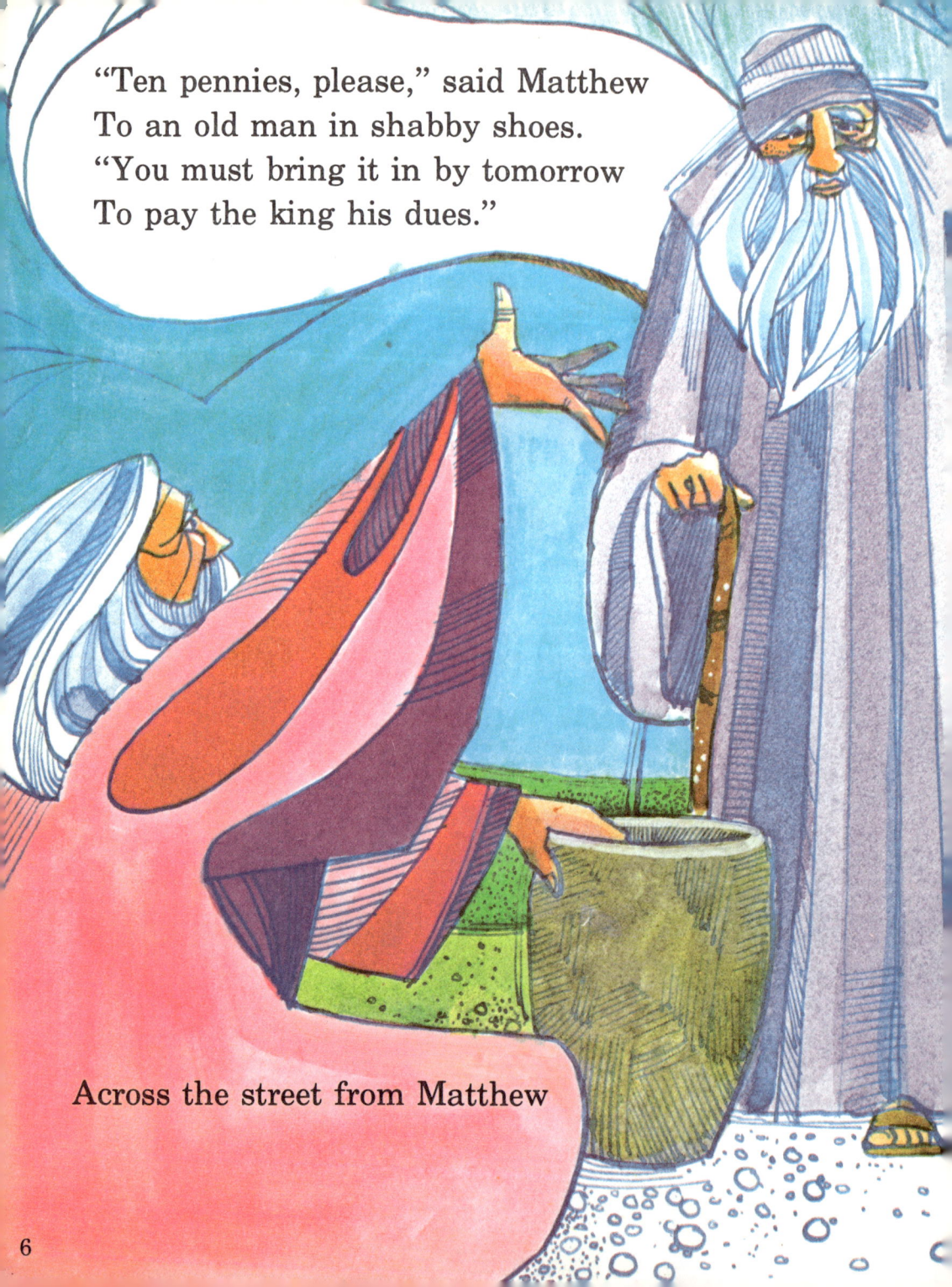

Across the street from Matthew

In a brand-new, striped tent
Ben Haran did the king's business,
Collecting taxes and rent.

In his tent at that very moment
A farmer with three children stood.
"I'll bring you the money, I promise.
I'd pay you if only I could."

The poor father begged and pleaded,
For he knew he never could pay
All the money the king demanded
No matter how long he'd delay.

Matthew slowly looked around him
At the people who stood in line.
Nearly all were poor and ragged.

Some were crippled, sick, and blind.

He looked at the tax collectors
With their robes so silky and fine.
They lived in the grandest houses
And drank the richest wine.

When Matthew went home to supper,
He was very sad at heart.

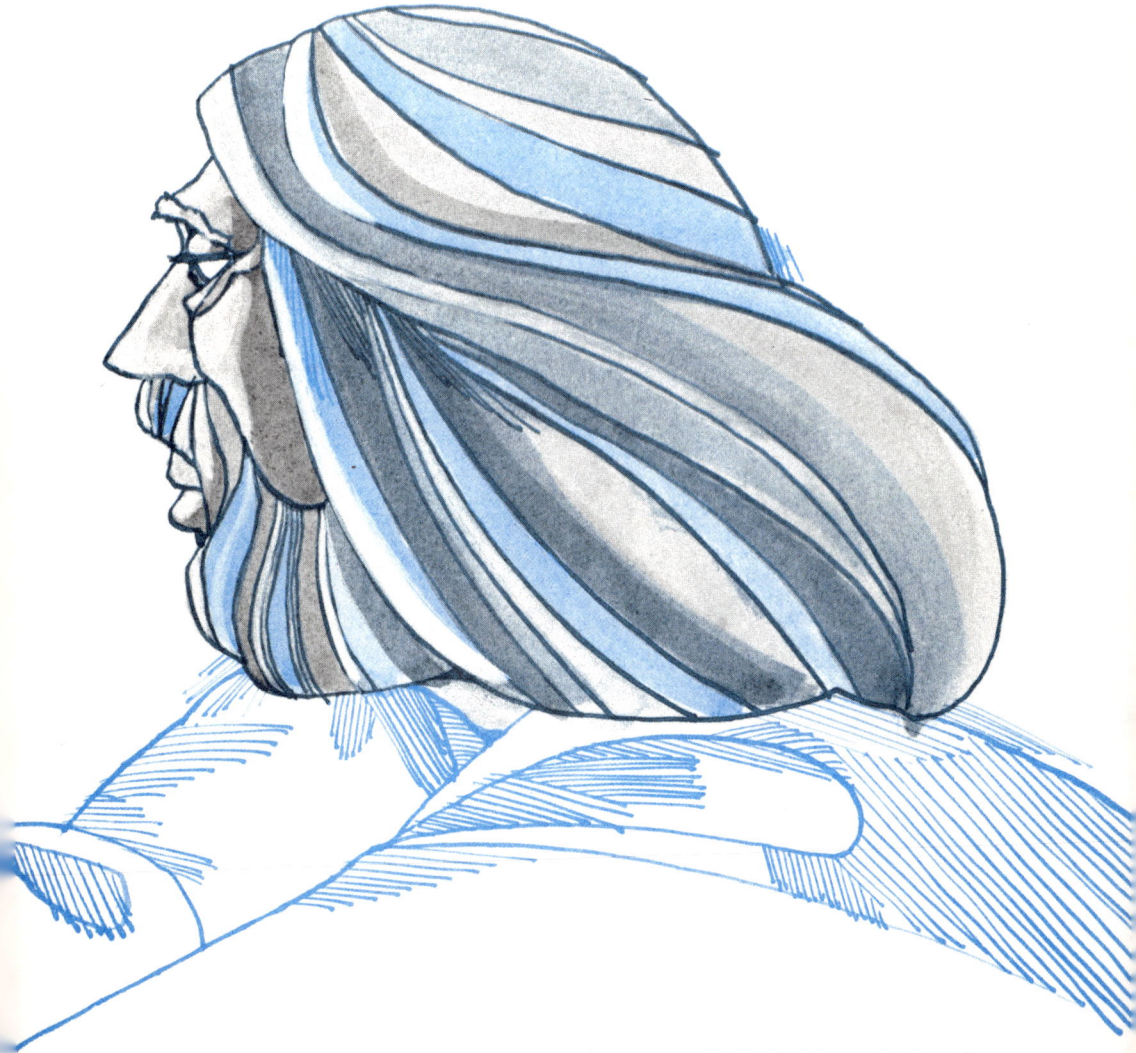

"I wish I could get a new job," he sighed.
"But I wouldn't know where to start."

On the grassy hills outside of town
At twilight Matthew went walking.
At the top of the hill a crowd sat still
While a bright young man sat talking.

"Be kind to one another," the gentle stranger said,
"Be good to those you hate.
For the person who thinks of himself the least
Is the person who will be great."

"What wonderful news," said Matthew,
"If only it could be true.

But a world like that can never be.
People do what they have to do.

"People have to get money for houses.
They have to work hard all day.
There is food to buy for the children,
And debts we have to pay."

"Look at the flowers," Christ told him.

"They do not work or sew,
But the clothes they have are more beautiful
Than anyone else's you know."

"Don't work for the treasures the world can give.
Silver and gold will rust.
But work for the treasures of heaven.
Give your life to the God you can trust."

That night Matthew lay in bed thinking,
  Wondering what he could do
    To be free of his old way of living,
      Wanting to start fresh and new.

In the hustle and bustle of noonday
Matthew worked by the city gate.
People dropped their coins in the cashbox,
But their eyes were filled with hate.

When suddenly Matthew saw Him
Standing tall above the crowd,
The man called Jesus was watching him.
"Follow me," Jesus said, clear and loud.

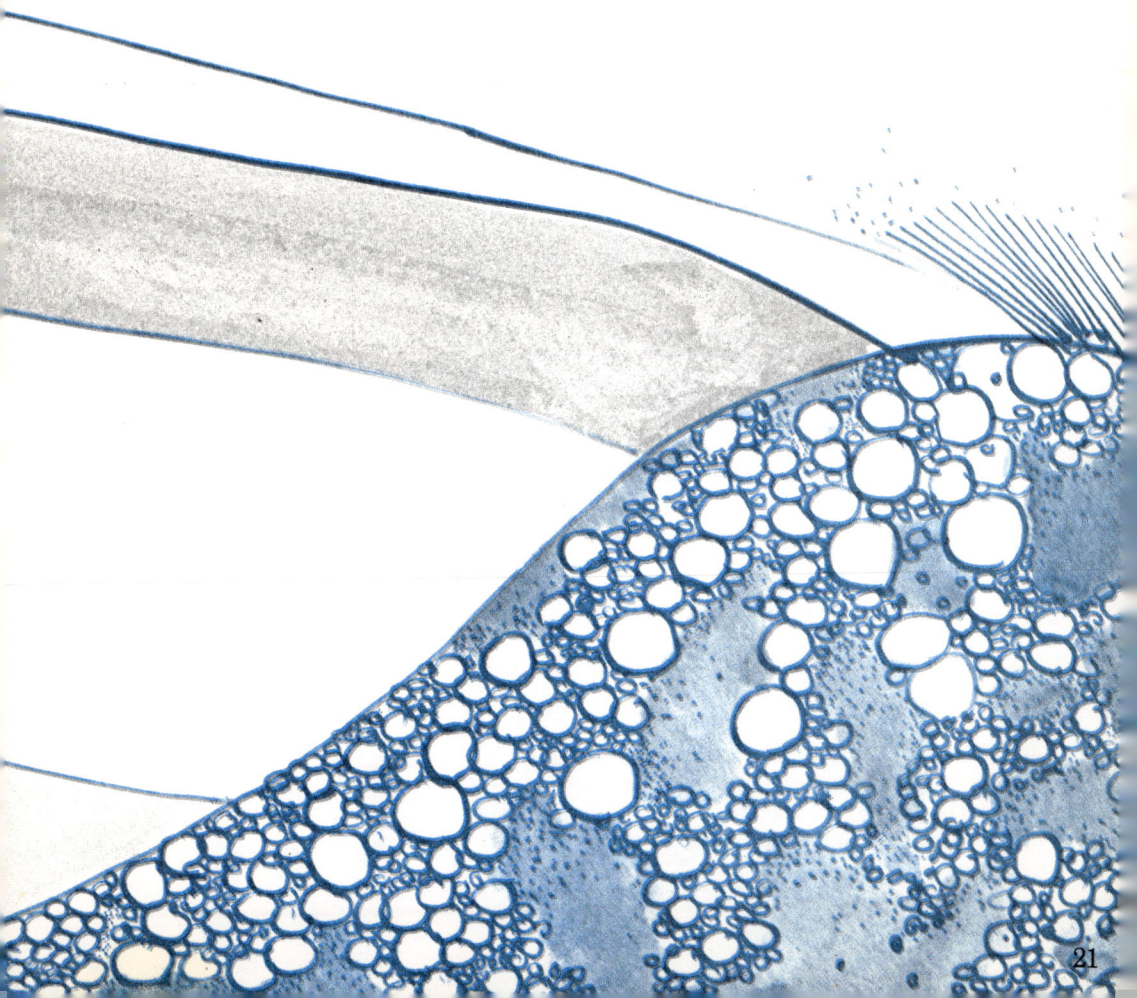

Matthew stood and pulled the curtains
And closed his collector's booth.
He had made up his mind and was certain.
He would follow the Master of Truth.

And the very next thing that he planned
Was a party for his old friends.
He arranged that the bad tax collectors
And his new friend Jesus attend.

Ben Haran arrived like a royal prince
In a carriage that flashed and rumbled.
Then Jesus and His disciples walked in.
And outside the Pharisees grumbled;

For they were angry with Jesus, who ate
And had parties with people who sin.
They didn't know that all people need
The forgiveness that Jesus would win.

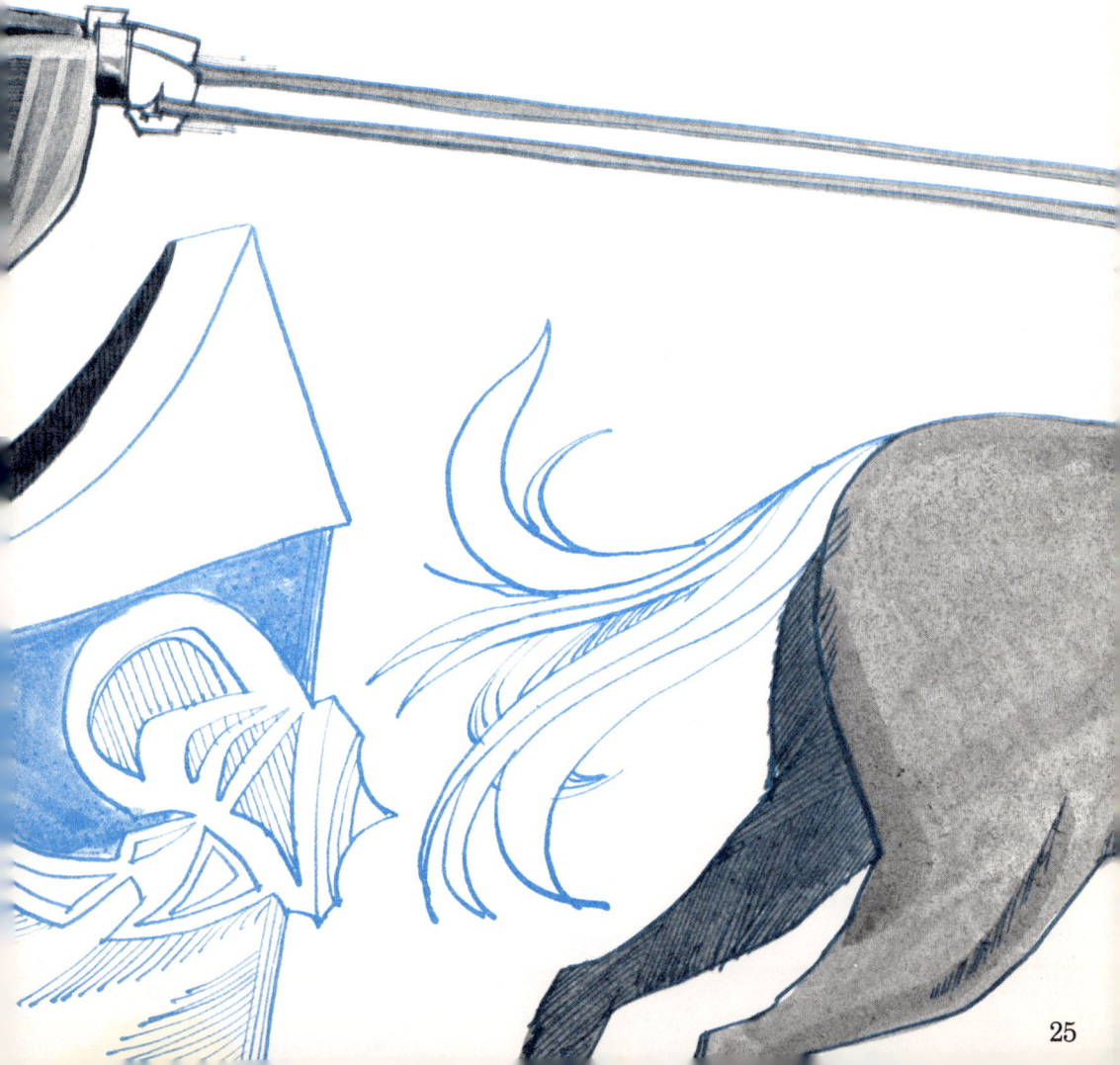

Inside the house Ben Haran ate
While Matthew began to speak,
"I've given up my tax job," he said
"To start a new job this week.

"I'm working for Jesus, the Son of God,
Beginning this very day."
"You must be crazy!" Ben Haran laughed.
"What made you decide that way?"

So Matthew tried to explain to all
Of the happiness Jesus can bring.
"I want to live the way Jesus lives:
To be kind, and happy, and sing."

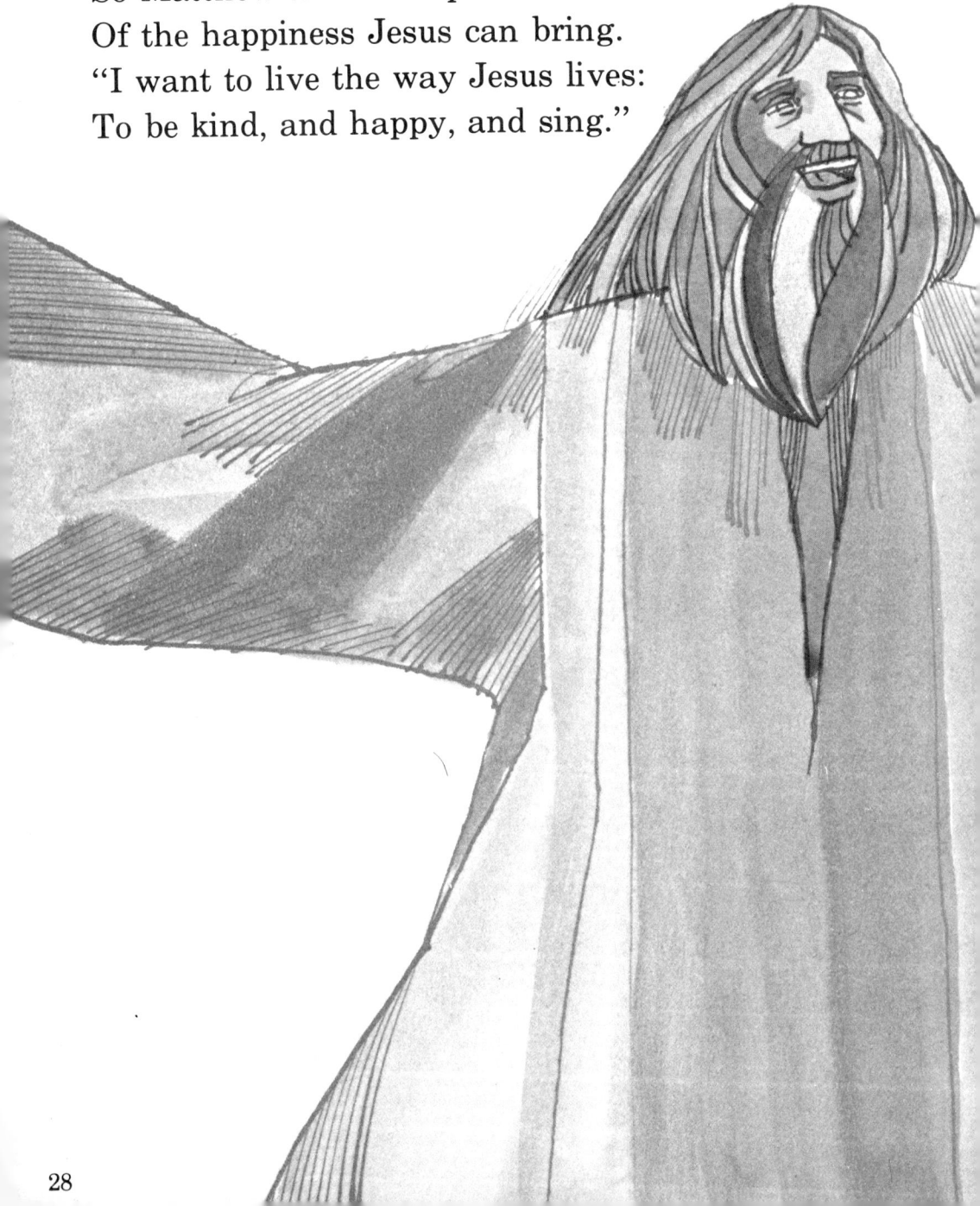

"I want to work for the things that matter—
The riches in heaven above.
I've found what I've always wanted," he said,
"Not houses or diamonds, but love."

And each day Jesus continued to show
The people how they should live.

And Matthew learned and never forgot
That the best part of love is to give.

DEAR PARENTS:

Matthew's conversion was about as radical as a conversion could get. Matthew collected enormous taxes from people already too poor. He was a taker. And he was part of a wealthy class of people despised by the poor but devout Jews.

When Jesus entered Matthew's life through His word—the same word He used to enter our lives—everything changed. No longer did Matthew take from the poor. Now he planned only to give, and to give the greatest riches of all: God's own love and forgiveness through Jesus. Matthew's change from taker to giver is nicely illustrated by his party.

However, when Jesus comes, He doesn't just give what we want Him to give to whom we want it given. No, Jesus gives happiness, love, and forgiveness to all people—to poor and rich, thief and honest person alike. When Jesus gives His happiness to anyone, that person must pass it on, for Jesus' gifts grow in people and through people.

In simple terms, point out to your children Jesus' message for true happiness—that we love one another. Help them understand that when Jesus' love enters our hearts, it can't remain dormant. Rather it explodes in us and compels us to love others as He loves us. In that way our lives become models of Christian living.

THE EDITOR